Don't miss the first hilarious title!

To my first grandchild—M.M.

For Mum, Nanny, Grandma, Trish, and Grannies everywhere—H.S.

First published in Great Britain and in the USA in 2016 by
Frances Lincoln Children's Books, 74-77 White Lion Street, London N1 9PF
QuartoKnows.com
visit our blogs at QuartoKnows.com

Text copyright © Margaret McAllister 2016
Illustrations copyright © Holly Sterling 2016

ISBN 978-1-84780-854-7

Illustrated with watercolour, pencil, and "printed" textures.

Printed in China

1 3 5 7 9 8 6 4 2

15 things NOT to do with a Grandma

Margaret McAllister

Illustrated by Holly Sterling

Frances Lincoln
Children's Books

A **grandma** is a wonderful person to have in your life. If you're really lucky, you might have two grandmas.

Follow these simple rules
to make sure every grandma
is a happy grandma.

Don't . . .

hide an **elephant** in
your grandma's bed.

Don't . . .

give her **squashed jelly beans** on toast for breakfast,

or put leftover **spaghetti** in her purse.

Don't . . .

wear her **underwear**
on your head,

or use her **make-up** on your teddy bear.

Don't . . .

race her on a **skateboard**.

(She might win.)

Don't . . .

give her a **crocodile** for her birthday,

or interrupt her doing **karate**.

Don't . . .

bang a **drum** to wake her up.

In fact, don't make any **loud noises**
when she's resting.

Don't . . .

ask her to read too
many **books** at once,

or forget to **share** her.

Don't . . .

send her up to the **moon** in a rocket.

Never . . .

swap her for a **giraffe**,

or someone else's grandma.

DO . . .

go for walks,

listen to her,

play,

sing,

hug *your* grandma,

help *your* grandma,

and most of all . . .

...love her. Lots.
She loves you!